This book belongs to:

....

Note to parents and carers

Read it yourself is a series of classic, traditional tales, written in a simple way to give children a confident and successful start to reading.

Each book is carefully structured to include many high-frequency words that are vital for first reading. The sentences on each page are supported closely by pictures to help with reading, and to offer lively details to talk about.

The books are graded into four levels that progressively introduce wider vocabulary and longer stories as a reader's ability grows.

Ideas for use

- Begin by looking through the book and talking about the pictures. Has your child heard this story before?

- Help your child with any words he does not know, either by helping him to sound them out or supplying them yourself.

- Developing readers can be concentrating so hard on the words that they sometimes don't fully grasp the meaning of what they're reading. Answering the puzzle questions on pages 30 and 31 will help with understanding.

For more information and advice,
visit www.ladybird.com/readityourself

Level 1 is ideal for children who have received some initial reading instruction. Each story is told very simply, using a small number of frequently repeated words.

Special features:

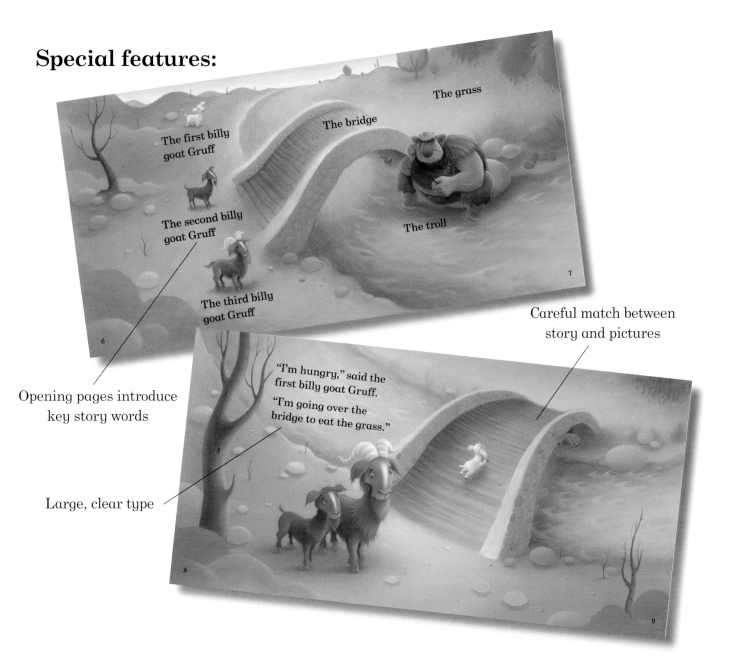

The grass

The bridge

The first billy goat Gruff

The second billy goat Gruff

The third billy goat Gruff

The troll

7

6

Careful match between story and pictures

Opening pages introduce key story words

"I'm hungry," said the first billy goat Gruff.

"I'm going over the bridge to eat the grass."

Large, clear type

8

9

Educational Consultant: Geraldine Taylor

A catalogue record for this book is available from the British Library

Published by Ladybird Books Ltd
80 Strand, London, WC2R 0RL
A Penguin Company

2 4 6 8 10 9 7 5 3
© LADYBIRD BOOKS LTD MMX
Ladybird, Read It Yourself and the Ladybird Logo are registered or
unregistered trade marks of Ladybird Books Limited.

ISBN: 978-1-40930-355-8

Printed in China

The Three
Billy Goats Gruff

Illustrated by Richard Johnson

The first billy
goat Gruff

The second billy
goat Gruff

The third billy
goat Gruff

The grass

The bridge

The troll

"I'm hungry," said the first billy goat Gruff.

"I'm going over the bridge to eat the grass."

8

Trip, trap!

Trip, trap!

Trip, trap!

Up jumped the troll.
"I'm going to eat you up,"
said the troll.

"Oh no," said the
first billy goat Gruff.

"Don't eat me. Eat the
second billy goat Gruff.
He's big and fat."

"I'm hungry," said the second billy goat Gruff.

"I'm going over the bridge to eat the grass."

Trip, trap!

Trip, trap!

Trip, trap!

Up jumped the troll.

"I'm going to eat you up," said the troll.

"Oh no," said the second billy goat Gruff.

"Don't eat me. Eat the third billy goat Gruff. He's big and fat."

"I'm hungry," said the third billy goat Gruff.

"I'm going over the bridge to eat the grass."

Trip, trap!

Trip, trap!

Trip, trap!

23

Up jumped the troll.
"I'm going to eat you up,"
said the troll.

"Oh no you're not," said the third billy goat Gruff. "I'm going to eat YOU up."

And that was the end
of the troll!

How much do you remember about the story of The Three Billy Goats Gruff? Answer these questions and find out!

- Why do the three billy goats Gruff want to go over the bridge?

- What does the troll want to do to the three billy goats Gruff?

- Where does the troll live?

Look at the pictures from the story and say the order they should go in.

A

B

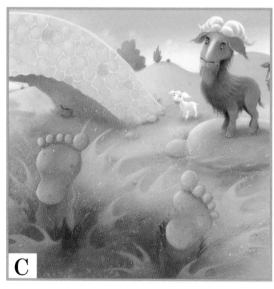

C

D

Read it yourself
with Ladybird

Level 1 — The Three Billy Goats Gruff

Level 1 — Cinderella

Level 1 — Little Red Hen

Level 1 — Goldilocks and the Three Bears

Level 1 — The Magic Porridge Pot

Level 1 — The Ugly Duckling

Level 2 — The Gingerbread Man

Level 2 — Sleeping Beauty

Level 2 — Sly Fox and Red Hen

Level 2 — The Three Little Pigs

Level 2 — Town Mouse and Country Mouse

Level 2 — Little Red Riding Hood

Level 3 — The Elves and the Shoemaker

Level 3 — Jack and the Beanstalk

Level 4 — The Pied Piper of Hamelin

Level 4 — The Wizard of Oz

Collect all the titles in the series.